Look for more

titles:

TWO of a kind™
Diaries
Twist and Shout

by Judy Katschke
from the series created by
Robert Griffard & Howard Adler

HarperEntertainment
An Imprint of HarperCollinsPublishers
A PARACHUTE PRESS BOOK

A PARACHUTE PRESS BOOK

Parachute Publishing, L.L.C.
156 Fifth Avenue
Suite 302
New York, NY 10010

Published by
HarperEntertainment

An Imprint of HarperCollins*Publishers*
10 East 53rd Street, New York, NY 10022-5299

TWO OF A KIND books created and produced by Parachute Press, L.L.C., in cooperation with Dualstar Publications, a division of Dualstar Entertainment Group, LLC, published by HarperEntertainment, an imprint of HarperCollins Publishers.

ISBN 0-06-059529-9

First printing: August 2004

Printed in the United States of America

Visit HarperEntertainment on the World Wide Web at
www.harpercollins.com

10 9 8 7 6 5 4 3 2 1

Chapter 1

Thursday

Dear Diary,

I'm so psyched! Ashley and I have been at Camp Rock 'n' Roll for two whole weeks. And here's the best part: We have *two whole weeks* left to go.

Camp Rock 'n' Roll is an all-girls camp in Pennsylvania. We're here to learn all about putting together a rock band. I've already made really cool friends—friends like Lark Maitland. Lark and I share all kinds of things: Bunk Elvis, for instance (all the bunks are named after rock stars)—and a serious love of soccer!

Today, before we headed over to the camp barbecue, Lark and I worked up an appetite on the soccer field. She has an awesome kick.

"Wow," I said as I watched her ball disappear over the trees.

"Where do you think it landed?" Lark asked, shading her brown eyes with her hand.

"Probably on the barbecue grill," I said. "I think I just heard a sizzle."

"Omigosh! The barbecue!" Lark exclaimed. "What if they already ran out of watermelon?"

"That would be the *pits*," I joked.

We ran to the barbecue so fast, Lark's long dark

hair bounced on her shoulders. Halfway there, she stopped. "I almost forgot," she said. "I have something for you."

She held up her arm to show me the studded leather bracelet I'd given her. "You made me a friendship bracelet in arts and crafts," she said. "So I made you one, too!" She reached into the pocket of her jeans, then dropped a bracelet with silver and turquoise beads into my hand.

"It's awesome!" I said. I slipped the bracelet on my wrist. "Thanks, Lark."

It's still hard to believe that Lark and I are friends. I've never known anyone who was rock royalty before. Lark's dad, Rodney Beecham, is a world-famous rock star with a huge mansion in England and a gazillion platinum records. But Lark is totally down-to-earth. We have tons of stuff in common. We both love sports, soggy cornflakes, and wearing sneakers all the time.

At the barbecue, Lark and I joined my sister, Ashley, and our other bunk mate, Janelle Chow, on the grass. Janelle's spiky black hair was stuffed into a backward baseball cap. She looked totally metal in her black shirt and studded bracelets. The only thing missing was her electric guitar.

"Hamburger," Janelle mumbled as she stared at her paper plate. "Hot dog . . . root beer . . . coleslaw . . ."

Twist and Shout

I stared at Janelle. Why was she acting so weird?

"Potato salad," Janelle kept mumbling. "Lemonade . . . barbecue sauce . . ."

"Janelle, what are you doing?" I finally asked.

"I was just thinking up more names for our band," Janelle said. "How about the Dill Pickles?"

Everyone at Camp Rock 'n' Roll is in a three-girl band. Lark sings and plays tambourine. Ashley and Janelle play electric guitar. I play a mean set of drums—well, more like four jumbo tin cans, three upside-down pails, and two aluminum buckets. My drums may look funky, but once I get the beat— watch out!

Janelle, Lark, and I are in a band we've been calling Crush. But before that it was The Diva Dollz, Xtreme—even Atomic Pizza!

"You guys change your band name more than most people change their socks!" Ashley joked.

"Let's stick with Crush, Janelle," I said. "'The Dill Pickles' sounds like some cartoon show."

"Fine with me," Janelle said. She picked up a corncob. "Now I can concentrate on the Battle of the Bands!"

The Battle of the Bands is the highlight of camp. The contest includes four different categories: harmony, vocals, choreography, and songwriting. The bands with the highest scores in the preliminary rounds compete for title of Best Band. So far, Ashley's band, Electric Pink, is tied with a band called Venus.

Even though her band was tied for first place, Ashley was too upset to be very happy about it. Her best friend, Phoebe Cahill, had just left camp, and I knew my sister blamed herself. Phoebe and Ashley were practically super-glued together at the White Oak Academy for Girls, our boarding school. But things didn't work out so well here at Camp Rock 'n' Roll.

"I'm getting seconds," Lark announced. "This potato salad is just too good." She stood up and strolled to the picnic tables.

"So, are you getting nervous about being in the music special?" Janelle asked me.

It's true, Diary! Lark's dad, Rodney Beecham, asked me to be in his TV special!

Sounds great, right? Just one problem: Lark was supposed to appear in that special with her dad. So now I feel weird that he picked me instead.

"I'm going to tell you something," I said in a low voice. "But don't repeat it to anyone else!"

"What?" Janelle said. She and Ashley leaned in close.

"I don't think I'm going to do the special," I said.

Janelle stared at me. "Have you been drinking

too much bug juice, Mary-Kate?" she said. "How can you *not* do the special?"

"Because Lark should be in it," I said. "Not me."

"But Rodney said she wasn't ready," Ashley said. "Her stage fright in the vocals round was too bad."

"Lark is really upset about that," I said. I told them more about Lark. How her parents are divorced. And the only time she sees her famous dad is when he plays a concert near her home in Santa Fe, New Mexico.

"Did Lark tell you she doesn't want you to do the special?" Janelle asked.

"No," I said. "She even made me promise not to drop out. She doesn't want her dad to know how hurt she really feels."

"How do *you* feel about it?" Ashley asked me.

I frowned. "Of course, part of me really wants to do it. It's a once-in-a-lifetime opportunity. I mean, being on TV with Rodney Beecham would be awesome! The other part knows that Lark should be performing with her dad, not me."

I reached up to brush my strawberry-blond hair out of my face and noticed the friendship bracelet Lark gave me. The bracelet decided it: My friendship with Lark should come first. "I'm calling Rodney Beecham tomorrow," I declared. "To tell him I'm *not* doing the TV special."

Dear Diary,

I think I'm the only one at camp who *didn't* have fun at the barbecue. I tried, Diary, I really tried, but I couldn't stop thinking about Phoebe.

Phoebe Cahill isn't just my roommate at school— she's my best friend. That's why I begged Phoebe to come to Camp Rock 'n' Roll with me. I even promised her that I'd always stick with her at camp no matter what.

But that was *before* I met Erin Verko. Erin is our bunkmate and she's totally hip. Her mom is the editor of *Teen Scene* magazine, so Erin came to camp with a rack full of cutting-edge clothes. (And Diary, you know how much I love clothes!) She's also really fun to hang out with.

I thought Erin was the best thing since quick-dry nail polish. I agreed with everything she wanted for our band, Electric Pink. I even started spending more time with Erin than Phoebe.

Phoebe tried to tell me how she felt, but I guess I wasn't listening. So Phoebe and I had a big fight, and then she left camp before dawn. Just like that!

Diary, I know I broke my promise to Phoebe. And I want to apologize, I really do—but I can't find her. All I know is that Phoebe is staying with her aunt in Philadelphia. The camp office won't give me her address or telephone number because it's "private information."

Without Phoebe, things aren't the same—especially with the band. I really missed her at music practice. Phoebe and I used to play our guitars side by side. She played lead. I played rhythm. It's hard to play rhythm by yourself! But music practice continued today—even though Electric Pink is now a duo instead of a trio.

"Since you're tied with Venus for first place, that'll be the band to beat," Jennifer said. Her long curly black hair hung over her shoulders. She wore her black GUITAR GODDESS T-shirt, jeans, and lots of chunky silver jewelry. "The focus of the next round is on choreography."

"Does that mean we have to outdance Venus?" I asked.

"Choreography isn't just about dancing," Jennifer said. "It's about presentation, so costumes and special effects count, too."

Jennifer showed us some famous rock videos. My favorite was one from the eighties called "Walk Like an Egyptian." Not only did the girls wear fancy Egyptian costumes, they came up with their own dance, too!

"Now, what will your band do?" Jennifer asked us.

Erin jumped up from her chair. She was wearing

red cargo shorts with a matching halter top. I recognized the outfit right away from the July issue of *Teen Scene*.

"I say we put down our instruments in the middle of the song," she said. "Then we shake it up like this!" Erin swung her arms and shook her hips. Her long blond hair whipped back and forth as she started to sing, "'When the world gets together, yeah, yeah, yeeeeeah!'"

It's a good thing Phoebe isn't here, I thought. *This is just the type of dancing she hates!*

"What do you think, Ashley?" Erin asked when she stopped. "I want you to be totally honest."

Honest? I took a deep breath, then said, "All that shaking is more like aerobics than dancing. In fact, just watching you made my teeth rattle. You reminded me of a bobble-head doll. In a speeding car."

"I didn't mean *that*, honest!" Erin said, her eyes wide with surprise.

Of course she's surprised, I realized. I had never disagreed with her before.

"Sorry, Erin," I said. "I didn't mean to hurt your feelings."

"It's okay," Erin said. "But for a minute there, you sounded like Phoebe."

Phoebe. She never agreed with any of Erin's

ideas. But just hearing her name made me miss her all over again.

Suddenly I knew exactly what I had to do.

Somehow I'm going to find Phoebe. And then I'm going to get her to come back to camp!

Chapter 2

Friday

Dear Diary,

Today our band, Crush, had our first dance practice in the music building.

"We can't come up with a dance number until we pick a song to sing," I said, twirling my drumsticks in my hands.

Our instructor, Bill, leaned back in his chair. He was wearing one of his Led Zeppelin tees and ripped-up jeans.

"You know, you *can* sing the same song you sang in the last round," Bill told us.

"You mean the song my dad wrote for us?" Lark asked.

"Why not?" Bill said with a grin. "How often does a first-time band get to play a song that a rock star wrote just for them?"

Lark started biting her thumbnail. Uh-oh. I knew what that meant. Lark always did that whenever she was worried.

The last time Lark sang her dad's song, in round number two, she was so nervous about pleasing him that she totally choked. She could barely get the words out of her mouth!

"Is it okay with you, Lark?" I asked.

"Sure." Lark shrugged. "Let's go for it."

I stood up and paced the room. "The song is called 'Butterfly Kiss,'" I said. "So what kind of dance number should we do?"

"I know!" Janelle said. "How about if we go outside and catch real butterflies? Then we can let them fly around the theater while we sing!"

"That reminds me of a scary movie I once saw," Lark said. "Millions of butterflies invaded this town. There were so many they started carrying off dogs and babies—"

Janelle groaned. "Next idea!"

I closed my eyes and thought of butterflies. When Ashley and I were around eight we caught a caterpillar and kept it in a jar. Days later the fuzzy-looking worm turned into a beautiful butterfly. "Hey!" I said. "Why don't we first flash pictures of caterpillars on the stage?"

Lark wrinkled her nose. "Caterpillars?" she repeated.

"Then what?" Janelle asked.

I pictured the whole thing in my head. "We can borrow a fog machine to make the stage look dreamy," I said. "Then the three of us can burst out onstage wearing colorful butterfly wings and funky makeup!"

"I like it, I like it," Lark said, nodding.

"And I can put gold streaks in my hair!" Janelle said.

I smiled at Janelle. She puts different-colored streaks in her hair for every round. Luckily they wash out!

"What do you think, Bill?" I asked.

"I think you totally rock, Mary-Kate," Bill said. "No wonder Rodney Beecham picked you to star in his TV special!"

Lark's smile turned into a frown. My stomach clenched when I saw her expression.

The door swung open. The camp owner, Stella Vickers, bopped into the room. She was dressed in cropped black pants and a red silk jacket. Her lips and nails were bright red, too.

"Guess what, Mary-Kate?" Stella exclaimed. "*Fave Rave* magazine wants to do a story about the lucky girl Rodney Beecham picked to star in his TV special!"

Did I just hear right? I wondered. Fave Rave *magazine only interviews teen celebrities—and now they want to interview me? Me? How awesome is that?*

"Mary-Kate!" Janelle whispered. "Didn't you tell Rodney that you weren't doing the special?"

I shook my head.

Diary, I'm so confused. What had started out as a dream come true was now turning into a big fat nightmare! Now, I not only have to tell Rodney I'm backing out, I have to tell Stella and *Fave Rave* magazine!

Things just got a lot more complicated.

Dear Diary,

This morning while everyone was in the music building talking about dance numbers and costumes, I was in the bunk, writing. No, not a new song for Electric Pink. An apology letter to Phoebe.

There was just one problem. I didn't have a clue where to send it!

The door flew open and Erin walked in. She was wearing pink shorts and a pink ruffled tank top—both from the May issue of *Teen Scene*.

"Ashley, why didn't you show up to talk about our dance number?" Erin asked. "We still have a great chance of winning Best Band. We got a score of nine out of ten in the last round, remember?"

But the only thing I remembered about that round was how Erin changed the words to Phoebe's song without telling us. And how I told Phoebe to forget about it. *Big* mistake!

"I can't stop thinking about Phoebe," I admitted. "I wrote an apology letter, but I don't know where to send it."

"Do you think this is *my* fault, Ashley?" Erin asked. "Do you think Phoebe left camp because I didn't listen to her ideas?"

"I didn't listen to her ideas, either, Erin," I admitted. "Maybe it's both of our faults."

Erin sat on the bed next to me and stared down at her sneakers.

"Look, Erin," I said, "in case Phoebe does come back, let's make a deal. Let's not be so quick to say bad things. Let's love one another's ideas for at least ten minutes. Okay?"

"Okay," Erin said. "And if Phoebe does come back, I promise I'll stay out of the way."

"Stay out of the way?" I said. "What do you mean?"

Erin shrugged. "You'd rather be friends with Phoebe than with me," she said. "That's okay. I can deal with it."

It was *not* okay! "Erin, I want us *all* to be friends," I said. "It's what I wanted from the beginning."

Erin's blue eyes opened wide. "Really?" she asked. "I thought you'd pick Phoebe over me because you've been friends for so long."

I shook my head. "No way. I really like you, too. I just wish that you and Phoebe could like each other."

"In that case, come on," Erin said. She grabbed

my hand and pulled me off the bed. "And bring your letter."

"Where are we going?" I asked.

Erin flashed a big smile. "To find Phoebe!"

We headed for the camp office. Gloria Stevens, Stella's secretary, was sitting at her desk. She had short black curly hair and big green eyes. Her lips were covered with dark purple lipstick.

"Hi, Gloria," Erin said.

We stood in the doorway while Gloria tacked another picture of Bryan Leland on her bulletin board. Bryan was the cute singer of Kooky Melon. Gloria had about a dozen pictures of Bryan on her bulletin board. One had a purple lip print on it!

"Are you here for Phoebe Cahill's address again?" Gloria asked. "I told you, Ashley. I can't give you her address. It's private information."

Gloria moved her computer screen so it didn't face me. Was Phoebe's information on that screen right now?

"We wanted to tell you that we just saw Bryan Leland," Erin said. "Going into Stella's office."

We did? I glanced down the hall to Stella's office. *Why didn't I notice?*

"Bryan is here? Here?" Gloria gasped.

"Sure," Erin said. "Stella knows all the major rock stars."

Gloria jumped up. She ran to the door and turned toward Stella's office.

"Gloria!" Erin said quickly. "You've got lipstick all over your teeth. Maybe you'd better go to the ladies' room and look in the mirror."

"Thanks!" Gloria said, turning the other way.

"And take your time!" Erin called after her. "You want to look your best for Bryan."

I grabbed Erin's hand. "What are we waiting for?" I asked. "I want to meet Bryan Leland, too!"

"Bryan isn't here," Erin whispered. "I just said that so we could lose Gloria!"

Erin quickly sat down at Gloria's desk and looked at the screen. "Are we lucky or what?" she squealed. "Gloria was just about to send an e-mail to Phoebe's aunt!"

Erin positioned her hands on the keyboard. "Quick, Ashley," she said. "Read me your letter to Phoebe."

I stared at Erin. What she wanted to do didn't seem right. "No, Erin," I said. "We can't—"

Erin cut me off. "Do you want to apologize to Phoebe or not?" she asked.

"Of course!" I said.

"Then read!" Erin ordered.

I yanked out the letter and I began to read out loud: "'Dear Phoebe, when I discovered you left camp, it was one of the worst days of my whole life. I don't blame you for being mad—'"

"Faster!" Erin said.

Faster? I took a deep breath and blurted everything out as fast as I could. "'I should have listened to you when you tried to talk to me. And most of all, I never should have broken the promise I made to you before we came to camp.'"

I stopped to take another breath. I froze when I heard footsteps in the hall.

"Someone's coming!" Erin said.

"Keep typing!" I urged. Then I read: "'I miss you, Phoebe. So please forgive me. And please come back to camp. Your best friend forever, Ashley.'"

The footsteps were getting louder. I shoved the letter back in my pocket. Erin stood up and clicked on Send. She moved away from the desk just as the door flew open.

"H-hi, Gloria," I stammered.

"Don't 'hi' me!" Gloria snapped. She planted her hands on her hips. "Stella said that Bryan was *never* here!"

"Oh, no!" Erin gasped. She swayed back and forth. "Then I must be seeing . . . rock stars!"

I tried not to giggle as I placed my hand on Erin's forehead. "You'd better get that checked out," I said.

We ran out of the main building, laughing the whole way.

"I can't believe it!" I said. "How did you learn to type so fast, Erin?"

"By having over a hundred friends on my buddy list!" Erin said. She put her arm around my shoulder. "Now Phoebe will definitely get your apology letter."

Oh, Diary, I sure hope so!

Chapter 3

Saturday

Dear Diary,

The butterfly wings Janelle, Lark, and I made in the arts and crafts cabin this morning are amazing. The paper we used is so thin, it's practically see-through. And the silver glitter and sequins add the perfect touch!

"How am I going to play my guitar in these things?" Janelle asked as we tried on the wings.

"Why don't you just . . . wing it?" I joked.

Ashley and Erin were in the arts and crafts cabin, too. Erin was stringing pink beads to make necklaces for their band. Ashley is great at costume design, so she was helping me with my wings.

"I've been thinking, Mary-Kate," Ashley whispered as she fitted me with my wings. "Maybe you shouldn't bail out of the TV special."

"Yeah," Janelle said. "What if Rodney still doesn't ask Lark to sing with him? Then it'll all be a big waste."

We stopped talking when Lark walked over.

"Guess what, Mary-Kate?" Lark said. "I heard on the radio that my dad is going on a European tour sometime around Christmas. Maybe you'll get to go, too."

"Why me?" I asked.

"Because you're going to be on his TV special," Lark said. "My dad sometimes tours with people who perform with him."

"Europe? Really?" I could see myself banging on my buckets, cans, and basins in front of Big Ben in London, the Eiffel Tower in Paris, the Colosseum in Rome. . . .

"I've never been to Europe before," I said.

"Me neither," Lark said.

I snapped out of my daydream and stared at Lark. "Didn't you ever go on tour with your dad?" I asked.

Lark shook her head. "He never asked me."

My butterfly wings sagged. How could I think of touring with Rodney when he'd never even asked his own daughter?

That did it. I left the arts and crafts cabin and headed straight to Stella's office.

"Can I help you, Mary-Kate?" Stella asked. She was watering the plants in her office. "Or should I say . . . Madame Butterfly?"

Whoops. I forgot I was still wearing wings! "I need to call Rodney Beecham about the TV special, please," I said. "Is this a good time?"

Stella's eyes lit up. "It's always a good time for Rodney," she said. "Let me give you his number."

Stella opened her black address book. She wrote

a telephone number on a sticky note and handed it to me. "I only have the number of his hotel in New York City," she said.

Someone knocked on the door. A counselor poked her head in. "Stella?" she said. "A camper just got her braces stuck on her trumpet mouthpiece!"

"Oh, great!" Stella moaned. "This is the second time this summer we've had a braces emergency!" She ran out of her office.

I picked up the receiver and dialed the number. "Metropolis Hotel," a man answered. "This is Jay."

"Hi," I said. "I'd like to speak to Rodney Beecham, please."

"You and a million other girls," Jay said. "Sorry. Mr. Beecham isn't taking any calls from fans."

"But I'm not a fan!" I exclaimed. "I mean . . . I am, but that's not why I'm calling. I'm performing in Rodney's next TV special."

"Right!" Jay laughed. "And I'm starring in Jennifer Lopez's next movie!"

Click.

I stared at the receiver. Jay had hung up!

I dialed the number one more time. When Jay answered again, I blurted out, "Jay, you've got to listen to me. Rodney Beecham *asked* me to be in his TV special—"

"You again?" Jay groaned. "Nice try. But it's not going to work."

Click.

"Great," I muttered. "How can I tell Rodney I can't do the TV special if I can't talk to him?"

Dear Diary,

Sunday morning I poured orange juice on my cornflakes. No, it's not some weird new health-kick. It's because I was tired from being up all night wondering if Phoebe got my e-mail. If she did, would she ever write me back? And if so, when? And what would she say?

If that wasn't enough—it's just three days away from round number three, and Erin and I still haven't decided on a dance number. Can things get any worse?

"All the other bands have their choreography numbers worked out," Jennifer said at practice. "What do we have so far? Zero. Zip. Zilch!"

Erin stared down at the ground. I felt bad, too. Up until then I'd had Phoebe on the brain—not music.

Jennifer is right, I thought. *We have to come up with something.*

I kicked my brain into gear. "Check this out," I

said. I turned on our radio boom box and found a pulsing techno-beat. Erin watched as I demonstrated moves from my dance class at school. I hopped from side to side, pumping my arms and legs in the air.

Erin tried copying me. "My knee keeps cracking," she complained.

"Then try this," I said as I fell into a split.

"As if!" Erin cried. "I definitely do not move that way."

I sighed. We couldn't win the choreography round if we didn't have a dance number. Any dance number!

"Okay," I said. "Let's go with *your* dance idea."

"You mean you'll shake it up?" Erin asked.

"Sure," I said, standing up.

"Okay." Jennifer pulled a stopwatch from her pocket. "First let's plan out some dance steps so I can time them."

"Okay!" Erin said. "Stand right next to me, Ashley, and do exactly as I do."

I watched Erin as she began to dance. "Let your hips sway and your arms jerk," Erin said.

I feel like a jerk, I thought as I copied her.

"Next, bend your head way, way over," Erin said. "As if you were a floppy rag doll."

I bent all the way forward—just like I do when I brush knots out of my hair!

"Now sway your head back and forth," Erin said. "And don't forget to make eye contact with the judges."

"Eye contact?" I laughed. "How can I with all this hair in my face?"

Erin straightened up. "Don't you like my dance number, Ashley?" she asked.

"It's not that I don't *like* it, Erin," I said, straightening up, too. "It's just that it's so . . . so . . . "

"Bubble-gummy?" a voice asked behind me.

Who said that?

I turned my head and gasped. Standing at the door with a big grin on her face was—"*Phoebe?*"

Chapter 4

Sunday

Dear Diary,

"Phoebe!" I shouted.

"Ashley!" Phoebe shouted.

We raced to each other with open arms.

"I'm sorry!" we both said at the same time.

I looked at Phoebe. "Why are *you* sorry?" I asked. "I'm the one who broke my promise. Not you."

"I know," Phoebe said. "But I spoke to my aunt Marie about everything that happened. She told me the promise you made was much too big to keep. I shouldn't have expected you to hang out with no one but me."

"But I should have known how upset you were," I said.

Phoebe shook her head. "And I should have made sure you knew how I truly felt," she said. "Instead of just leaving."

Then Phoebe looked straight at Erin.

Uh-oh, I thought. *What if Phoebe is still mad at Erin?*

"Erin, I'm sorry I blamed you for putting that red sock in my wash," Phoebe said. "When I spoke to my mom, she said she'd packed a pair of red socks in my duffel bag. The sock that turned my clothes pink was really mine."

"No way!" Erin exclaimed.

"It's true." Phoebe laughed.

"Are you back at camp now, Phoebe? For good?" I asked.

Phoebe nodded. "I missed you guys," she said. "And besides," she added with a grin, "my aunt Marie has six cats that kept me up all night."

"Okay, okay," Jennifer said. "Now that we've had our warm and fuzzy moment, can we please choose a dance number?"

Erin looked Phoebe up and down. "Not until Phoebe tells me where she got that awesome dress," she said.

Phoebe glanced down at her white minidress. It had a tomato soup can print on it. "This dress is vintage nineteen sixty-six," she said. "My aunt lent me tons of sixties clothes to bring back to camp."

"How did she get them?" I asked.

"Aunt Marie wore all kinds of mod clothes when she danced on *American Grandstand*," Phoebe explained.

Erin gaped at Phoebe. "That is so cool. *American Grandstand* was the hottest teen show in history."

"And look at the dance steps Aunt Marie showed me," Phoebe said. She moved her hands as if she were climbing a tree. "This is called the Monkey."

Phoebe showed us how to dance the Skate, the Shingaling, and the Mashed Potato. Somewhere in the middle of the Philly Dog, I got the most amazing idea! "Hey, you guys," I said. "Why don't we turn Electric Pink into Electric Pink a Go-Go?"

"Electric Pink . . . a go-go?" Erin repeated.

"The mod look is hot this year," I explained. "And we still haven't decided on a dance number, so—"

"So let's go totally sixties!" Phoebe cried.

"Sweet!" Erin said.

"We can sing a song from the sixties, wear sixties clothes, and do a bunch of dances from the sixties, too," I suggested.

"I'll call my mom," Erin said. "Maybe she can mail us some old issues of *Teen Scene* magazine. So we can see what hairstyles and makeup girls wore back then."

Jennifer loved the idea, too. She offered to flash psychedelic designs on the wall while we performed.

"Wait," Erin said, looking at her watch. "We're supposed to love one another's ideas for ten minutes."

"All I need is ten *seconds*," I said.

"Me too!" Phoebe said. "I love it."

"Great," Erin said.

"You mean *groovy*!" I giggled.

Phoebe, Erin, and I spent the whole afternoon planning our dances and our new look. But the best part is, Diary, everyone is getting along. *At last!*

Dear Diary,

This afternoon, Janelle and I had a few minutes alone in our bunk.

"I have to get out of that music special," I said. I told her about my failed phone call with Jay earlier. "But how *can* I when I can't reach Rodney?"

"Of course you can't reach Rodney Beecham," Janelle said. "He's a superstar."

"Then who else can I try to call?" I asked.

Janelle tightened her guitar strings as she thought. "What about Rodney's manager?" she suggested. "The one who came with Rodney when he visited the camp last time?"

Of course! My forehead wrinkled as I tried to remember the woman's name. "Dorothy . . . Dolly . . ." I snapped my fingers. "Doris! Her name is Doris! She gave me her business card with her phone number in case I had any questions."

"Perfect!" Janelle said. "Where is it?"

"I think I stuck it in my jeans pocket," I said,

reaching into my pocket. Nothing. "I guess I was wearing my other jeans that day. The ones I put in my laundry bag."

Janelle pointed out the window. "You mean the one going to the laundry today?" she asked.

"Huh?" I glanced out the window. A guy with a cap was loading the campers' laundry bags into a big truck.

"Janelle!" I squeaked. "I have to get Doris's card back. Before it shreds in the wash!"

I raced out of the bunk. "Stop!" I shouted as I ran after the truck. "I left something in my pocket!"

I wasn't alone. Mandy Plotnick was chasing the truck right behind me. Mandy had left her favorite lip gloss in her pocket.

We stopped running as the truck drove out of the camp gate. We stared after it, panting.

"There goes my only tube of Cherry-Berry," Mandy said.

And there goes Doris's phone number—and my only chance to reach Rodney I thought.

As I trudged back to the bunk I dug my hands into the pockets of my hoodie. That's when I felt something. It was stiff like cardboard and rectangular like a business card.

A business card?

Hey, wait a minute, I thought.

I pulled out the card and smiled. It *was* Doris's business card and telephone number!

Am I lucky or what? I thought. *I guess I never put it in my jeans after all. Now let's see if I'm lucky enough to reach Doris—and get out of the TV special!*

Chapter 5

Monday

Dear Diary,

You should have seen us this morning. Electric Pink arrived in the practice room wearing the clothes we chose for the round tomorrow. Phoebe wore an orange vinyl miniskirt with a matching vinyl jacket. Erin picked out a black sleeveless dress splashed with yellow and white daisies, and daisy-shaped earrings, too. I'm wearing white bell-bottom hip-hugger pants and a cropped red jacket.

"You guys are stylin'!" Jennifer said. "Erin, I love those mod daisies on your dress."

"So do the bees." Erin groaned. "They chased me all the way here."

We all gathered around the stereo to choose a song. After listening to tons of CDs of sixties music, we decided on a tune called "Twist and Shout."

"Let's *dance* the Twist, too," Phoebe said.

"How do you do that?" I asked.

"You just twist at the waist," Phoebe said. "And grind your foot on the floor like you're stepping on a bug!"

"Ewww!" Erin said with a giggle.

"You guys stay here and practice," Jennifer said. "I'll look into some special effects."

As Jennifer pulled the door open, Skye Martell, Tori Seever, and Abigail Bederman from the band Venus fell into the room. They were wearing silver space suits and space boots.

"Were you guys listening in?" Jennifer demanded. "It's not cool for bands to spy on other bands."

"You're Jennifer, aren't you?" Skye asked. "Your guitar playing *rules*. No wonder they call you Guitar Goddess!"

Jennifer's face softened. "Thanks."

Then Skye lowered her voice and said, "Don't tell our instructor, Tina, but we really wish *you* were our instructor."

"That is so sweet," Jennifer gushed. She left the room, and the girls from Venus strolled over to us.

They weren't smiling sweetly anymore.

"Hi," I said. "I'm Ashley. This is Phoebe. And Erin."

"We know," Abigail said.

"Let's cut to the chase," Skye said. "You may be ahead of us, but not for long."

I blinked hard. "Excuse me?"

Skye flipped her long red hair over her shoulder. "We're the real deal," she said. "We sound better than you, have better costumes than you, and we probably dance better than you, too!"

"*And* we're using a bubble machine for special effects," Tori said, her dark eyes flashing.

"Can you top that?" Abigail asked with a mean grin. "I don't think so!"

Diary, I couldn't believe my ears. Were these girls snooty or what?

"Don't think you're such hot stuff, Electric Pink," Skye said. "Venus is going to win the Battle of the Bands—no matter *what* it takes."

Venus left the room and slammed the door. Erin, Phoebe, and I turned to one another, our mouths open in shock.

"Who do they think they are?" Phoebe cried.

"Why did they say all those nasty things about our band?" Erin exclaimed.

"Who knows?" I said. "Unless they're trying to psych us out."

"Psych us out?" Phoebe asked nervously. "I don't get it."

"Venus is getting nervous because they know we're good," I explained. "That's why they're trying to scare us. So we don't do well in the next rounds."

"Scare us?" Phoebe cried. "Hah!"

"Let them try," Erin declared. "Nobody scares Electric Pink."

The three of us high-fived with knuckles. Knuckles meant business. Then we all shouted, "Electric Pink rules!"

And with our groovy sixties costumes and cool song, we are going to *prove* it!

Dear Diary,

This morning after breakfast I raced to Stella's office to call Doris.

"When you talk to Rodney's manager," Stella said as I sat down, "ask her if Rodney can mention Camp Rock 'n' Roll in his song."

Oh, great, I thought. *Stella really wants the camp to be a part of Rodney's TV special. How can I get out of it with her listening in? I can't kick her out of her own office.*

The door flew open, and an instructor rushed in. "Stella, one of the bands is planning on using pyrotechnics!" he said.

"You mean *fire*?" Stella gasped. "Absolutely not! Once I finish with Mary-Kate, I'll come and set them straight."

"No!" I blurted. "I'm fine by myself. Really!"

"Really?" Stella asked.

"Really," I said firmly.

"Well, okay, then," Stella said, standing up.

Stella and the instructor hurried out of the office. I pulled out Doris's card and dialed the number. After a few rings—"Doris Gavin here!" a voice snapped.

"Um, Doris," I said. "This is Mary-Kate Burke. I just wanted to—"

"Mary-Kate!" Doris interrupted. "I was just going to call you. I need your dad's name for the release form."

"It's Kevin. Kevin Burke," I said. "But I really need to talk to you. It's about the TV special."

"Oh, we're excited, too, Mary-Kate," Doris said. "Hold on—I have a call on another line."

An old Rodney Beecham song came on the line while Doris put me on hold. I was just starting to hum it when—

"I'm back," Doris chirped. "Now, what did you want to tell me, Mary-Kate?"

I took a deep breath and said, "I don't think I can do the TV special, Doris. You see—"

"Sure you can do it," Doris cut in. "You have just the right energy. Rats—there's my other line again."

"Wait!" I said. But Doris put me on hold—again!

A different Rodney Beecham song came on. But I didn't want to listen to music. I wanted to get out of the TV special once and for all.

"Me again," Doris said. "That was Rodney's yoga instructor. He wanted to know how many sticky mats he should bring on our next tour. As if I care."

"Doris—" I started to say.

"I'll mail that release form to your dad ASAP,

Mary-Kate," Doris said. "And we'll see you when we come up to camp next week for the TV shoot. Bye, now."

Click.

I can't believe it! I thought. *Getting out of a rock TV special is just as hard as getting into one!*

I stuffed Doris's card back into my pocket and wondered if it was worth calling her back later. As I walked out of the main building, Janelle ran over. "So?" Janelle asked. "Did you do it? Are you out?"

"No." I sighed. "Rodney's manager is too busy to talk. And I'm sure I still won't be able to get to Rodney, either."

"Maybe what you need is a password," Janelle said.

"A what?" I said.

"Rodney's secret password," Janelle said. "Sometimes it's the only way to get through to a famous rocker."

"How do you know?" I asked.

"I've been trying to call Jim Nolan of Gag Reflex for about a year," Janelle said. "No luck."

Janelle pulled a notepad and pen from her guitar case. She put the case on the ground and got ready to write. "If Rodney Beecham had a secret password," she said, tapping her chin with her pen, "what would it be?"

"Rodney's last CD was called *Poison Ivy*," I said.

"Poison ivy!" Janelle began to write. "Itch . . . scratch . . . rash. Rash! What a cool name for our band! Itchy Rash—"

"Janelle," I cut in. "Focus."

"Sorry," Janelle said. "Rodney did a cereal commercial once."

"Cereal," I said. "Crunchy . . . flaky . . . milky . . . "

"He has a dog," Janelle added. "Bark . . . fetch . . . stay!"

I know what you're thinking, Diary. Guessing Rodney Beecham's secret password won't exactly be a piece of cake.

Hey, wait a minute. Cake . . . cupcake . . . cookie . . . I'd better add those to my list!

Chapter 6

Tuesday

Dear Diary,

This is it! Round three—choreogra-phy! Phoebe, Erin, and I spent the whole morning putting on sixties makeup and teasing our hair to the max.

"When do I stop?" I asked, fluffing my hair with a fine-tooth comb.

"When it reaches the ceiling," Phoebe joked.

Erin showed us how to paint our eyelids with liquid eyeliner. Next we borrowed some of Erin's pale pink and white lipstick. They were the "rage" back in the sixties.

"How did you get all this cool retro makeup, Erin?" Phoebe asked.

Erin smiled at us with pink pearly lips. "Not only does my mom get me free clothes from *Teen Scene* magazine, she gets me free makeup," she said. "And free hair stuff. And free nail polish. And a free subscription—"

"We get the picture." I giggled.

I blotted my lipstick with a tissue, then gave myself one last look. Ready! "Let's hurry," I said, "or we'll be late!"

We grabbed our instruments and raced to the camp theater. Jennifer waved to us from the aisle.

"Good luck!" she called. "I'll be up in the lighting booth working the special effects."

I knew what the special effects would be: pink and black spirals all over the stage wall. Very psychedelic!

A few guys called "roadies" were already up on the stage. Their job was to set up all the amps, microphones, and instruments before each band played.

"Welcome, rockers!" Stella said as she walked across the stage with a handheld microphone. "Today's round is all about choreography!"

Everyone cheered.

"But first, let's give it up for our judges," Stella said. "Clarence Meekins, Sophie Amir, and Terrence Boyle!"

The judges waved from their table.

Sophie looked her totally glam self in a black sleeveless dress and huge silver hoop earrings. Clarence was wearing his usual backward baseball cap. Sophie and Clarence are tough judges but always have something nice to say. Then there's Terrence. Terrence "the Terror" Boyle is known for being honest. A little *too* honest!

"The first band up will be Fresh Start," Stella said. "Girls, the stage is yours!"

The three girls of Fresh Start hurried onstage.

One sat down behind a set of drums. One stood at a keyboard. Another picked up a trumpet.

After an opening drum solo, Fresh Start began to sing: "'I want candy! I want candy!'"

When they weren't singing or playing their instruments, Fresh Start wowed us with their awesome moves. Their legs and arms moved in perfect sync. One girl spun on her head so fast, she became a blur!

Fresh Start got huge cheers. And high scores from Clarence and Sophie. But as for Terrence . . .

"If this were a gymnastics competition, I would have given you a ten," he said. "But since you all sang flat, you get a five from me. Sorry."

"Ouch!" Phoebe whispered.

"Thanks, Fresh Start," Stella said. "Now let's put on our space gear and blast off to Planet Venus!"

"Venus!" Phoebe whispered. "Let's see if they're as good as they say they are."

First Skye, Tori, and Abigail moonwalked across the stage. Next they broke into their robotic dance steps. Then they played their instruments while pictures of planets and stars flashed all over the theater. The bubble machine was a big hit, too.

"'Cosmic Cutie up so far, send me your love on a shooting star!'" they sang.

"I'm pretty sure the judges won't like it," Erin

whispered. "Whoever heard of bubbles in space?"

The judges *did* like it. A lot. They gave Venus a *nine*! One point away from a perfect ten!

"All riiight!" Stella said. "Now let's get back to Earth and hear from the gals of Electric Pink a Go-Go!"

"I can't believe we have to go after Venus," Phoebe whispered. "They were so good."

"So are *we*!" I whispered back.

Phoebe, Erin, and I walked onto the stage. Once we were set up, Jennifer gave us a thumbs-up from the projection booth.

"One, two," Erin called out. "One, two, three!"

Phoebe and I strummed our guitars and began to sing, "'Shake it up, baby, now. Twist and shout. Twist and shout!'"

After a few minutes our recorded music began to play. It was our cue to dance!

Phoebe and I put down our guitars. Erin stepped away from her keyboard. The three of us danced the Monkey, the Skate, and the Jerk. I was just about to switch to the Mashed Potato when pink and black spirals swirled all over the stage. I tried to keep dancing, but all those swirling lights were making me dizzy. Soon it felt as if the whole stage were swirling—faster and faster and faster!

Diary, I could barely feel the floor under my feet.

My eyes started to cross. My stomach started to churn.

Omigosh! I thought in a panic. *I'm going to barf!*

Dear Diary,

I didn't know what to do! There I was, sitting in the third row of the theater, watching my sister turn a sickly shade of green! "Ashley is going to hurl," I whispered to Lark.

"Oh, no!" Lark gasped.

"Are you going to do something?" Janelle whispered.

Just then, Jennifer switched the effects to giant mod hearts and daisies. Luckily they didn't swirl! Phew!

Ashley made it through the whole song, and Electric Pink got a score of nine from the judges!

"That's what I call moving to the groove," Clarence said. "Good job, Electric Pink."

"For a minute there I thought I was back in the sixties," Sophie said. "You girls were on fire."

"Your swaying was very dramatic, too, Ashley," Terrence said. "Nice touch. Very nice touch."

I looked at my friends and cracked a smile.

Stella tallied the judges' scores. "All riiiight!" she declared. "Electric Pink gets a nine, too!"

Twist and Shout

After two more bands it was time for Crush.

"Let's do it!" Janelle said.

Wearing our butterfly wings and glittery make-up, we slipped behind the stage curtain. We waited while Bill projected shots of squirmy caterpillars all over the stage. The roadies worked the fog machine, creating a fine mist. Janelle strummed a chord, and we burst through the curtain.

"'When you're away, the thing I miss,'" Lark sang. "'Is your great smile and your butterfly kiss!'"

Diary, we gave it all we got. But when our song was over, the judges only gave us six points.

"So what if our wings kept knocking together?" Janelle complained later in the bunk. "It didn't bother me."

"Well, it bothered the judges," I said as I started taking off my glitter makeup.

"So did our pictures of the caterpillars," Janelle said. "I heard Terrence tell Sophie that caterpillars gross him out."

"Spiders gross my dad out," Lark said.

I froze with the cotton ball in my hand. Could "spider" be Rodney's secret password? "Spiders, huh?" I said slowly. "Are there any other bugs your dad doesn't like?"

"Not that I know of," Lark said.

"Any bugs he *loves*?" I asked. "How about ladybugs? Does he have a favorite animal? A favorite ice-cream flavor?"

"No," Lark said, staring at me.

Janelle shot me a grin. She must have known I was still trying to figure out Rodney's password. But Lark didn't have a clue.

"Are you okay, Mary-Kate?" Lark asked. "You've been acting kind of weird these last few days."

"Actually, I could use some fresh air," I said. "I'll be right back!"

I grabbed Rodney's New York telephone number, my list of passwords, and raced to Stella's office.

"*Another* call to Rodney Beecham?" Stella asked when she saw me. She shrugged. "Go ahead."

I dialed the number as fast as I could.

"Metropolis Hotel," a voice answered. "Jay speaking."

It's Jay, I thought. *The same guy from a few days ago.*

"Can I help you?" Jay asked.

"Um—spider?" I blurted. "Spider *web* . . . tarantula . . . creepy crawly . . . Little Miss Muffet . . . itchy . . . wire-haired terrier?"

"Is this some kind of joke?" Jay asked.

"No!" I cried. "Queen Elizabeth . . . pistachio?"

Click.

"He did it again," I wailed. "He hung up."

Twist and Shout

I forgot I wasn't alone. I looked up and saw Stella staring at me. "Is everything okay, Mary-Kate?" she asked.

"Fine," I said, forcing a smile. "Everything's fine."

But I knew it wasn't.

Lark should be doing this TV special. But it looks like *I'm* doing it—whether I want to or not!

Chapter 7

Wednesday

Dear Diary,

Because we worked so hard on the last round, Stella gave us the whole day off. That meant no practice or music classes. Some campers practiced with their bands, anyway. Some slept late and just relaxed.

Phoebe, Erin, and I did both. We hung out by the lake, but we practiced guitar chords and talked about the next round. The *final* round!

"We showed those girls from Venus," Erin said. She leaned back against a tree. "We were as good as they were."

"Better!" Phoebe said.

"Let's forget about Venus and think about the next round," I said. "I say we stick with the sixties look. That went over big."

"Thanks to Phoebe," Erin said with a smile.

I smiled, too, as I strummed my guitar. It was supercool to have us all get along!

"The final round focuses on songwriting," I said. "Should we start coming up with a new song?"

"We don't have to," Phoebe said. She pulled a piece of paper from her guitar case. "I just happen to have a new song right here."

"What a surprise!" I joked. Phoebe had been writing songs nonstop since she got to camp.

"This song is kind of serious, but in a fun way," Phoebe said. "It's called 'Great to Know You.'"

"What's it about?" Erin asked.

"It's about opening your heart to new people," Phoebe explained.

New people? I thought. *As in . . . Erin?*

Phoebe strummed her guitar as she sang. When she was finished, she looked up and said, "What do you think?"

She glanced nervously at Erin.

Uh-oh, I thought. *What if Erin doesn't like it? What if Phoebe and Erin start fighting again?*

Erin grinned. "I love it!" she said.

"You do?" Phoebe asked.

"What a *relief!*" I cried. I quickly shook my head. "I mean—what a coincidence—I love it, too!"

"It's great to sing about friends," Erin said. "We can even flash pictures of new friends here at Camp Rock 'n' Roll!"

"This time we should wear go-go boots," Phoebe said. "They're little white boots that all the cool girls wore in the sixties. I think I saw some in the costume cabin."

"What are we waiting for?" I asked. We raced to the costume cabin.

Linda, the costume counselor, was busy ironing The Corral Chicks' denim skirts. She looked totally cool in khaki flared pants, a black tank top, and colored bangle bracelets up to her elbows. Linda put aside her iron and helped us pick out three pink minidresses and three pairs of white go-go boots.

"I've never worn vintage boots," Erin said. "What if the girl who wore these before had sweaty feet?"

"Mod girls in the sixties never sweated," Phoebe joked. "They were too cool!"

"Good one," a voice said behind us.

I spun around. Skye, Tori, and Abigail were walking into the cabin.

Venus!

"Those boots are so slammin'!" Skye said. "Are you wearing them in the next round?"

I kept my mouth shut because I didn't trust them. Were they here to put down our band again?

"They are so perfect for your look," Skye said. "But then everything Linda picks out is perfect."

"You think?" Linda said.

"For sure!" Tori said. "In fact, we were just going to ask you if you have any bracelets we can wear."

"Come to think of it," Linda said. "I think I have some silver bracelets in the back room."

"We'll wait," Tori said sweetly.

Twist and Shout

When Linda was in the back, the girls of Venus stopped smiling.

"Okay, we tied for that last round," Skye said. "But you were just lucky."

"The *next* round is what really counts," Abigail said.

I shrugged. "May the best band win," I said.

"And that is going to be us!" Skye said. "We're older than you. And we're better than you, too."

"*And* we have a bubble machine!" Tori said. She stuck out her tongue like a little kid!

The three girls walked into the back room. Phoebe, Erin, and I exchanged stunned looks.

"Are they super mean or what?" Erin asked.

"Should we tell somebody?" Phoebe asked.

I thought about it, but shook my head. "They didn't really do anything to us," I said. "Besides being nasty."

"Thanks, Linda!" Skye's voice boomed from the back. "These bracelets are perfect. You *are* a fashion-genius!"

"And you guys are so sweet," Linda's voice gushed.

I rolled my eyes.

Skye, Tori, and Abigail were kissing up to the instructors and the counselors. No one had any idea what Venus was *really* like!

"Even if we did complain to the counselors and instructors about Venus," I said, "who would believe us?"

Dear Diary,

After practicing our new song, Janelle took her guitar outside. Lark and I stayed in the bunk to write some letters.

"I'm almost done. How about a game of soccer?" Lark asked.

"Sounds great!" I licked my last envelope and tossed it aside. I noticed a book on Lark's bedside table.

"What are you reading?" I asked, nodding toward the book.

Lark held it up for me to see. A picture of Rodney Beecham was on the cover. The title of the book was *Rodney Beecham: Feed Me with Rock!* "It's my dad's autobiography," Lark said. "It came in the mail yesterday." She tossed it to me.

"Wow!" I said, opening the book. "He even signed it for you."

"Big deal," Lark said. "I'd rather get to know my dad in person than in some book. And do you believe there's just one paragraph about me? One dumb paragraph!"

Diary, I couldn't take it anymore. Lark's dad was making her so miserable.

"Why don't you just get real with your dad, Lark?" I asked. "Tell him that you want to be in his TV special!"

"But I *don't* want to be in the TV special," Lark said.

I stared at Lark. "You don't?"

"It's not about the music, Mary-Kate," Lark said. "It's about spending more time with my dad."

"It is?" I asked.

Lark nodded. "But maybe it's better that I hardly see him," she said. "He would probably think I was a drag."

"How can you be a drag?" I asked.

"My dad loves to perform. I don't," Lark explained. "He loves flashy clothes. I like T-shirts and jeans. He loves attention. I get shy around lots of people."

"In other words . . . you and your dad have nothing in common," I said.

"Zero!" Lark said.

While Lark looked for her sneakers, I flipped through Rodney's autobiography. As I was about to put the book on Lark's bed, it suddenly hit me: If I could help Lark connect with her dad, she would finally be happy.

And I'd be happy being in the TV special. We'd both get what we really want!

All I had to do was find something that they had in common.

"Can we play soccer later, Lark?" I asked. "I want to check out your dad's new book."

Lark's shoulders dropped. She looked disappointed. I wasn't sure if it was because she was looking forward to soccer, or because she was afraid I was becoming one of her dad's obsessed fans. But, I reminded myself, it was all for a good cause.

She shrugged. "Sure. Knock yourself out."

I carried the book outside. I found Janelle lying on the grass, bopping to the beat of her Walkman.

"Janelle!" I said, waving the book over her face. "Check it out!"

Janelle pulled off her headphones. Her eyes went wide as I explained everything.

"That's why I have to read Rodney's biography," I said. "It's the only way I'll find out what Rodney likes to do. And I hope Lark will like doing the same things."

Janelle whistled as she flipped through the book. "This book is three hundred and fifteen pages," she said.

"I've never read such a thick book before," I admitted.

"I can help you look through it," Janelle offered. "But if we're going to go through Rodney's whole life, we'd better get started. He's been around over forty years!"

I opened the book and flipped through the pages. "Check out these pictures in the middle," I said. I pointed to a shot of a woman holding a baby. They both had big dark eyes. "I'll bet that's Lark and her mom."

Janelle peered over my shoulder as I turned more pages. I stopped at a chapter called "The Great Outdoors" and read out loud: "'Being on tour for months can make a bloke batty. So when I get to my castle I pull on my hiking boots, whistle for my wire-haired terrier Oliver, and take long walks on my estate.'"

"What do you know?" Janelle said. "Rodney likes to hike."

"Janelle, that's it," I said, shutting the book. "Lark and her dad can go hiking together."

"Wait a minute," Janelle said, shaking her head. "How do you know if Lark even likes hiking?"

"I don't," I admitted. "But there's only one way to find out!"

Chapter 8

Later Wednesday

Dear Diary,

I know I already wrote you today, Diary, but I just have to tell you what happened.

It wasn't easy talking Lark into taking a hike. All she wanted to do was play soccer.

"I promise we'll play soccer after the hike," I said for the fourth time.

"Okay," Lark finally said. "But since when are you so into hiking?"

Gulp! I'd never been hiking in my life. So I had to think of something fast. "Um, this *is* the country," I said. "So why shouldn't we be one with nature? Or, in our case—two?"

It was late afternoon and getting cool. We pulled on our hoodies and headed for the woodsy part of camp.

"Shouldn't we bring a flashlight?" Lark asked as we entered the woods. "Or canteens?"

"Maybe we should drop breadcrumbs, too!" I joked. "These woods aren't that deep. And we won't be long."

I hope! I thought.

Twigs and leaves crunched under our sneakers

54

as we trekked into the woods. I could hear crickets chirping and birds twittering up in the trees.

"Hey! I have an idea. Maybe you can go hiking with your dad when he gets here," I said. "Wouldn't that be neat?"

"Are you serious?" Lark scoffed. "My dad hates the outdoors."

I stopped walking and stared at Lark. "He . . . what?" I asked.

"My dad hates the outdoors," Lark repeated. "He's always getting bitten by mosquitoes. He once even got poison ivy in his own backyard. Why do you think he named his last CD *Poison Ivy*?"

"But . . . the book said your dad loves hiking!" I said.

"The book lied," Lark said. She slapped her neck and started scratching. "Now I'm getting attacked by mosquitoes, too. Just great!"

I heard a loud snap. And a screech.

"What was that?" Lark whispered.

"Probably just nature sounds," I said.

Lark started scratching her leg. "I think I've had enough of nature," she said. "Can we go back to camp now?"

Boy, Diary, did I goof! Not only does Lark hate hiking—her dad does, too.

There's got to be something Rodney likes to do, I

thought. *Something that doesn't call for flashlights or bug spray!*

Dear Diary,

This morning after arts and crafts, Phoebe, Erin, and I carried our new sixties outfits from the costume cabin to the music building. Each practice room has its own clothing rack so the bands don't have to keep their costumes in the bunks.

"I can't wait to show Jennifer our outfits," I said. "Especially the go-go boots. They are so stylin'."

We hung up our minidresses and lined up our boots against the wall. Then we headed to the mess hall for lunch. Our bunk counselor, Ivy, sat across from me. Instead of eating spaghetti and meatballs like the rest of us, she just nibbled on a roll.

"What's up, Ivy?" I asked. "Don't you feel well?"

"I have no appetite," Ivy said. "The girls from Venus left the most awesome cookies in the counselors' lounge this morning. Abigail's mom sent them in a care package."

Venus? I looked sideways at Phoebe and Erin.

"Those girls should win an award for the nicest band," Ivy said. "Don't you think?"

No one said a word. I glanced over at the next table. Abigail was winding her spaghetti on a fork.

She looked right at me and smiled. A slow, sly smile. Then Skye speared a meatball on her fork and waved it back and forth.

"Why is she doing that?" Phoebe whispered.

"They're still trying to psych us out," I whispered. "Let's just ignore them."

After lunch, Bunk Elvis played a mean game of softball with Bunk Tina Turner. Mary-Kate scored two home runs! Then we all headed to the music building for band practice.

Jennifer was waiting for us in our music room. She pointed to the rack. "Amazing costumes," she said.

"Wait until you see the boots," I said.

We kicked off our sneakers and pulled off our bulky socks. Then we stuck our feet into the boots.

Squish!

"Ewww!" Phoebe cried.

"My boots have worms inside them!" Erin exclaimed.

"Worms?" Jennifer gasped.

Yick! My own boot was filled with some kind of cold, squishy, squiggly mush. Diary, I practically gagged—that's how grossed out I was!

We yanked our boots off and gasped. Our feet were covered with red and brown goop that smelled like meat sauce. When we tipped our boots over, clumps of spaghetti and meatballs plopped out on the floor.

"Gross!" I cried.

"Who would do this to our vintage go-go boots? Now they're totally ruined!" Phoebe wailed.

I remembered the look Abigail gave me in the mess hall while she was winding her spaghetti. And that meatball Skye waved at me. I had a pretty good idea who had dumped the spaghetti and meatballs into our boots. But Erin spoke up before I did.

"The girls from Venus have been acting pretty snooty lately," Erin said. "It must have been them."

Jennifer shook her head. "The girls from Venus are so sweet," she said. "They wouldn't do something like that."

"But—" Erin started to say.

"In fact," Jennifer went on, "Abigail helped me restring my guitar. She's good at it. And fast, too."

I groaned under my breath. It was no use. Venus had already kissed up to Jennifer!

"Do you want to report this prank to Stella?" Jennifer asked.

"That's okay," I said. "We'll deal with it."

Erin and Phoebe stared at me.

"Why don't you wash your feet while I take these boots to the costume cabin?" Jennifer said. "Maybe Linda can have them cleaned."

Twist and Shout

Phoebe, Erin, and I left meat sauce tracks in the hall as we walked to the bathroom.

"Ashley, why *don't* you want to tell Stella?" Phoebe asked. "We can't let Venus get away with this."

"We're Electric Pink—not Electric Rat Fink," I explained. "And we don't have any proof that Venus did it."

"Proof-shmoof." Erin narrowed her blue eyes. "We should get *even*. A prank for a prank, that's what I say!"

That didn't fly with me. Once we got even, Venus would do something to top us. And we would just go back and forth trying to get revenge.

"Getting even isn't what we're about," I said. "We'd only be stooping to their level."

I knew the Battle of the Bands would be tough. But I never dreamed it would be an all-out *war*!

Chapter 9

Friday

Dear Diary,

Today was the first rainy day at camp. So instead of the volleyball game and canoe lessons that were scheduled for this morning, the whole camp played Rock 'n' Roll bingo in the mess hall.

But not me! I stayed in the bunk and read about Rodney Beecham.

"I can't believe you talked me into missing Rock 'n' Roll bingo for this," Janelle said. "It's like doing homework."

We sat on my bed in Bunk Elvis, flipping through the book I held on my lap.

"I'm on a mission, Janelle," I said. "There *has* to be something Rodney likes that Lark likes, too."

"Hey," Janelle said, pointing to a page. "It says that Rodney is good at arm wrestling. Do you think Lark is good at that?"

I pictured Lark arm-wrestling the muscled roadies in the mess-hall. "I hope not!" I groaned.

I turned the page. The next chapter was called "Chip off the Ol' Rock-Block." It was about Rodney's father.

"According to this, Rodney's dad used to play the trumpet in his army band," I said.

"So?" Janelle asked. "We want to know what Rodney likes doing—not his dad."

"Wait," I said. "It also says that Rodney's dad used to take him rowing when he was a kid."

"He did?" Janelle asked.

I read the paragraph out loud: "'Rowing with my dad is one of my best memories. So whenever I feel low—all I have to do is *row*!'"

I looked up and stared at Janelle. "The camp has rowboats out on the lake," I said. "Maybe Lark can go rowing with her dad when he visits."

"Did you ever see Lark row before?" Janelle asked.

"No," I said. "But there's always a first time."

As soon as it stopped raining, I looked for Lark. I found her on the playing field dribbling a soccer ball. It was muddy, but Lark didn't seem to mind.

She kicked the ball over to me. "Offense or defense?" she asked.

"Um," I said, putting my foot on the ball, "instead of playing soccer . . . can we go boating?"

"Boating?" Lark asked. "Really?"

"Sure!" I said. "Did you ever row before?"

"Never," Lark admitted.

"Oh, Lark, you have to try it," I said. "Ashley and I went rowing with our school last spring. We had a blast."

Lark looked up and said, "What if it starts raining again? The sky looks pretty gray."

"A little drizzle won't hurt us," I said.

Lark smiled. "Okay. If you really want to. But after that—"

"Soccer!" I said. "I know."

Lark and I headed down to the lake, where a lifeguard was on duty. He gave us permission to take a rowboat out on the water.

After putting on orange life jackets, Lark and I pushed a small wooden rowboat into the water. The boat rocked as we carefully stepped in and sat down.

"I'll take the oars first," I said. "Then you can give it a shot."

Lark gripped the sides of the boat as I rowed away from the shore.

"Does your dad like to row?" I asked.

"I think he used to go boating with my grandfather," Lark said. She bit her thumbnail. "But he never took me rowing."

He will soon! I thought with a grin.

"Why don't you take the oars for a while, Lark?" I asked. "You'll get the hang of it."

Lark looked nervous as we carefully switched seats. She sat in the middle and took the oars. I sat at the bow—that's sailor-talk for the front of the boat.

I showed Lark how to grip the oars and dig them into the water at the same time.

"Am I doing it right?" Lark asked as she rowed.

I turned and gulped. Our boat was heading straight toward the diving dock!

"Lark—steer away from the dock," I said.

"How?" Lark cried.

"Pick up your left oar!" I said. "And dig in with your right—"

CRUNCH! Too late. The front of our rowboat got stuck underneath the dock!

"I stink at this." Lark groaned.

"It's no big deal," I said.

We leaned over and tried freeing the boat. It was so wedged in, it didn't budge. And as if things weren't bad enough, it started to rain. Not just a little drizzle, but a sky-opening, cloud-gushing downpour!

The lifeguard started shouting directions at us. Other campers and counselors stood on the shore, watching.

"This is soooo embarrassing!" Lark cried.

It was even more embarrassing when the lifeguard rowed his own boat over to rescue us.

"I don't ever want to see another rowboat in my life," Lark muttered as we were rowed back to shore. "Ever!"

Our feet sloshed in the mud as we walked to Bunk Elvis.

Maybe Lark was right, I thought. *Maybe she and her dad don't have anything in common. . . .*

And maybe I should mind my own beeswax!

Dear Diary,

Most of the bands spent the rainy day playing Rock 'n' Roll bingo. But not Electric Pink. We decided to practice all morning.

"We have to be ready for the Battle of the Bands on Monday," I said. We dodged raindrops on our way to the music building.

"And for *Venus*," Erin added.

Jennifer had to supervise bingo, but she left us her tape recorder so we could hear what we sounded like.

"Let's run through the whole song," I said as we set up in our music room. I plugged in the tape recorder and when we were ready I clicked the record button.

"'Great to know you, great to know you,'" we sang. "'Where would I be if I didn't meet you?'"

Somewhere in the middle of the song there was a knock on the door, and Linda opened it. "Sorry to interrupt, but I cleaned your go-go boots," she said.

"They're in the costume cabin if you want them."

"Thank you so much," Phoebe said. She turned to us and said, "Let's grab them before anyone can get to them again."

"Good idea," I said.

We left our instruments and followed Linda to the costume cabin. Our boots were neatly lined up on a table—and they looked clean.

"No more spaghetti and meatballs," Linda said, holding out a boot. "No saucy smell, either. Take a whiff."

The last thing I wanted to do was sniff a boot—even if it *was* my own. "That's okay," I said. "I believe you."

The three of us carried our boots back to the music room. This time we shut them safely inside a cabinet.

"Let's pick up the song from the top," I said.

Erin sat at her keyboard. Phoebe and I lifted our guitars. We both started to strum. But the notes we were playing were totally mixed up!

"Hey!" I said. "My chords are all screwy!"

"So are mine," Phoebe said.

We quickly inspected our guitars.

"Omigosh!" I gasped. "Our strings were all switched!"

Erin rubbed her fingers together. "My keys feel

all slimy," she said. "Ewww—someone rubbed butter all over them!"

"Somebody ruined our instruments," Phoebe declared.

The three of us stared at one another. "Venus!" we shouted in unison.

"But how could they switch your strings so fast?" Erin asked. "We were only gone around half an hour."

"Jennifer said that Abigail is great at changing guitar strings," Phoebe said. "And fast, too."

That did it, Diary. Now I was mad!

"I don't care if we *are* snitches," I said. "We're going to tell Stella everything."

We marched to the main building. We knocked on the door of Stella's office. A girl's voice sweetly said, "Come in!"

I opened the door and froze. The girls of Venus were scurrying around Stella's office. Tori was watering Stella's plants. Abigail was refilling the coffeemaker, and Skye was stuffing envelopes.

"What are you doing here?" I asked.

Stella glanced up from her desk. "They just came by to help me around the office," she said. "Isn't that nice?"

"We couldn't think of a better way to spend a rainy day," Skye said with a smile.

"Stella does so much for us," Abigail said. "Isn't it time we did something for her?"

"You guys are the best," Stella said. Then she looked at us. "Now . . . what can I do for you?"

My mouth opened to speak, but nothing came out. Why bother telling Stella about the boots and the instruments? Now *she* thought the girls of Venus were total angels, too!

"It's okay," I said, shaking my head. "It's not important."

Phoebe and Erin shook their heads, too. We filed out of the building. Once outside, I turned to Phoebe and Erin. "I think it's time," I declared.

"Time for what?" Erin asked.

I took a deep breath and said, "Time to *get even!*"

Chapter 10

Saturday

Dear Diary,

Phoebe wanted to switch Venus's  sheet music. Erin wanted to crack eggs in their space boots. But I had another idea. . . .

"Let's do something to their precious bubble machine," I said. "That's what they're so proud of."

So last night while everyone was asleep, Phoebe, Erin, and I sneaked out of our bunk. But just as we were about to run to the music building, Phoebe grabbed my arm. "Wait!" she whispered. "There's a counselor on night duty. She's sitting on the porch of Bunk Elton John."

We ducked behind a tree and peeked out. Natalie Berg was sitting under a porch light, reading a magazine.

"How are we going to get past her?" I whispered.

"I have an idea," Erin whispered. She picked up a stone and tossed it into the bushes next to Bunk Elton John. It made a sharp rustling noise.

Natalie jumped up. "Is someone there?" she called.

I held my breath as Natalie walked to the far side of the porch with a flashlight. As soon as she was busy inspecting the bushes, I whispered, "Let's go!"

The three of us raced across the campgrounds to the music building. We couldn't go too fast because Erin kept tripping in her pink fuzzy slippers.

Once inside I flipped on the light switch and looked around. Venus's silver space costumes were hanging on a rack. Their instruments were standing against the wall. And their bubble machine was set up on the floor—right where we hoped it would be.

Phoebe picked up a plastic bottle next to the machine. The label read, BUBBLE MACHINE SOLUTION. "This must be the stuff that makes the bubbles," she said.

"And this must be where it goes," I said, opening a small compartment on top of the machine. There was a drop of blue bubble solution still inside.

"Here's the switch," Erin said, pointing to a dial. "Maybe we can turn the bubble machine to High while Venus is practicing."

"We can't switch the machine while they're in here," I said. "They'll see us."

"How else can we pump up the bubbles?" Phoebe asked.

Good question! I paced the room as I thought.

"Mary-Kate and I had a bubble blizzard once," I said. "In our kitchen back in Chicago."

"What happened?" Phoebe asked.

"Our dad goofed." I giggled. "He put liquid dish soap into the dishwasher by mistake. As soon as he turned it on, the whole kitchen was flooded with bubbles."

"Too bad there isn't a dishwasher in this room," Phoebe said, laughing. "We could have done the same thing."

"Hey, wait a minute!" I said. "We can put dish-washing liquid in the bubble machine."

Phoebe smiled and said, "So when they turn it on—"

"Bubble attack!" Erin squealed.

It was the middle of the night, so we tried to not laugh too loud. "It's a great plan," I said. "We just need some dishwashing liquid."

The kitchen was locked, so we waited until the morning.

As everyone filed into the mess hall for breakfast, I turned to Ivy. "Phoebe, Erin, and I would like to practice during breakfast" I said. "We already ate some granola bars in the bunk."

"Okay," Ivy said. "But you'll be missing French toast with cinnamon sugar and maple syrup."

My mouth watered. But the French toast would have to wait. We were on a mission!

Phoebe, Erin, and I ran around the mess hall to

the kitchen. We were going to ask the staff if we could borrow some dishwashing liquid, but we didn't have to—there were two bottles of Swishy Dishy on the kitchen windowsill.

"Lemon . . . or antibacterial?" Erin asked.

"Any!" I said.

Erin grabbed the bottle of lemon-scented soap and stuck it under her sweatshirt.

We raced to Venus's practice room. Erin filled the bubble machine with Swishy Dishy—all the way to the top.

"We'd better go," Phoebe whispered. "Breakfast will be over soon."

"But I want to watch when they turn on the bubble machine!" Erin said.

"Okay," I said. "We'll wait in our practice room until we hear Venus come. Then we'll peek through their door."

Phoebe, Erin, and I went to our practice room. We left the door open a crack and listened. It wasn't long before we heard voices in the hall.

"Let's run through the song before Tina gets here," Skye was saying. "We don't need her."

I smiled at my friends. "It's showtime!"

We glanced down the hall to make sure Venus was in their room. We snuck up to the door and peeked through the small glass window.

The girls were already playing. Tori was on drums, Abigail was on bass, and Skye was on electric guitar.

"'Your love is a million light years away,'" they sang. "'But nothing on Earth can stand in our waaaaay!'"

The bubble machine! I thought. *What about the bubble machine?*

I sighed with relief when Abigail switched on the machine with her toe. Only a few bubbles popped out. Until—

WHOOSH! Thick foam gushed out of the machine onto the floor. Soon, the whole room turned into a bubble storm!

"Shut that thing off!" Skye shrieked.

"I did!" Tori screamed. "The bubbles won't stop!"

Phoebe, Erin, and I laughed as the girls tried to fight the out-of-control bubbles.

"It worked," I said. "Our plan worked!"

"What *plan*?" a voice demanded.

Phoebe, Erin, and I spun around. Stella was standing behind us.

Uh-oh! I thought. *We're toast!* And I didn't mean French toast with cinnamon and sugar!

The door swung open, and bubbles poured out. Skye, Tori, and Abigail ran out of the room. Their clothes and hair looked wet and sticky.

Twist and Shout

Skye glared at us. "They did it, Stella!" she said. "They messed with our bubble machine."

"Why, what makes you say that?" Erin asked sweetly.

Skye pointed to the bottle of Swishy Dishy in Erin's hands.

"Oh!" Erin gulped.

"Camp Rock 'n' Roll doesn't stand for pranks," Stella said. "I'm afraid Electric Pink is out of the Battle of the Bands. You're disqualified."

Dear Diary,

When I heard Ashley's news, I was stunned.

"I wish you'd told me what you were planning to do, Ashley," I said. "I would have talked you out of it."

Ashley and I were alone in the bunk. We sat on the floor and leaned against the bed frames.

"Too late now," Ashley said, and sighed. "We blew it."

Lark suddenly ran into the bunk. "They're getting a soccer game together outside," Lark said. She grabbed my hand and pulled me up. "The teams are called the Rolling Stones and the Supremes."

The three of us ran outside. Campers were already sitting on the grass around the main field.

Ashley found Phoebe and sat next to her. Lark and I ran over to Beverly, the counselor-ref.

"You'll be midfielder for the Stones, Mary-Kate," Beverly said. "Lark, you'll play forward for the Supremes."

Beverly handed out bandannas—red for the Stones, blue for the Supremes. We tied them around our necks.

After the kickoff, Lark excelled as usual. She dribbled the ball like a pro. When the ball was kicked in her direction, she headed it and sent it flying across the field!

"Suuuper!" a voice shouted.

I knew that voice anywhere!

I turned and saw Rodney Beecham. He was wearing a black T-shirt, white drawstring pants—and a huge smile.

What's he doing here? I wondered. *He isn't supposed to come until tomorrow!*

"Owww!" A girl on my team named Kimberly stumbled to the ground, rubbing her calf.

Beverly called a time-out and hurried over. "It's just a cramp," she said. "But you'd better sit it out, Kimberly."

Beverly turned to the campers on the grass. "Who wants to sub for Kim?"

Nobody answered. Until—

"Come on, mates!" Rodney shouted. "Let's show those Supremes we've got game!"

Rodney ran onto the field. He picked up the ball and shouted, "What are we waiting for? Let's play ball!"

Rodney Beecham plays soccer? I thought. *No way!*

Lark looked surprised, too. "Dad?" she said.

"Here you go, love," Rodney said. He shot the ball over to Lark. In a flash, her stunned face turned into her game face, and she kicked the ball way across the field!

"Suuuper!" Rodney cheered again.

You should have been there, Diary. Rodney played an amazing game, and so did Lark. In the end, Lark shot the winning goal kick, and the Supremes won!

"That's my girl!" Rodney shouted. He lifted Lark on his shoulders and paraded her around the field.

"Yaaaay, Lark!" I cheered with everyone else.

Lark had never looked so happy. And I was happy, too. That's because Lark and her dad *do* have something in common, Diary. Something that isn't even in the book.

Soccer!

Chapter 11

Sunday

Dear Diary,

I can't remember ever being so
bummed out. All the other campers
were practicing for the Battle of the
Bands tomorrow, but not Electric Pink.

Phoebe was on her bed, reading a book of poetry.
Sad poetry—to match her mood. I lay on my own
bed, staring at the ceiling. Erin tried to keep busy by
alphabetizing her lip gloss.

"All that hard work," I said. "For nothing."

"It's Venus's fault that we were disqualified, you
know," Erin said. "They started it."

"We didn't have to get even," I pointed out.

"Let's just talk to Stella and tell her every rotten
thing Venus did to us," Phoebe said.

"We still don't have any proof," I said, shaking
my head. "And everyone thinks those girls are
angels—including Stella."

The bunk door opened. Jennifer walked inside
wearing her GUITAR GODDESS T-shirt, jeans, and a
very long face.

"I'm just as upset as you guys," Jennifer said. She
held out a cassette tape. "Here. I found this inside
my tape recorder."

I rolled off my bed and took the tape. "It's the

recording of our last practice," I said. "The day our guitar strings were switched."

"We must have left it in the tape recorder," Phoebe said.

"Now you can have a souvenir of your band," Jennifer said, forcing a smile. She left the bunk.

"Just trash the tape, Ashley," Erin said. "What good is it now?"

I looked at the tape. The words ELECTRIC PINK were written with a pink marker on the label. "No," I said, shaking my head. "Electric Pink was a great band. We should be proud of our music."

I borrowed Janelle's Walkman and slipped the cassette inside. Then I lay on my bed, put on the earphones, and clicked the green Play button.

Our song "Great to Know You" began to play. For a rehearsal, it sounded pretty good.

Then I heard Linda's voice on the tape. That was when she came into the room to tell us about our boots. I could hear us put down our instruments and leave the room.

We must have forgotten to switch off the tape when we went to the costume cabin, I realized.

Then other voices came on the tape.

"I thought they'd *never* leave!"

"Hurry up, Abigail. Switch the guitar strings while I grease up the keyboard!"

"Tori, give me hand. I'll tell you what to do."

"If this doesn't psych out Electric Pink, I don't know what will."

I sat up straight on my bed. I clicked off the tape recorder and turned to my friends. "You guys," I said. "I think we can go to Stella now!"

Dear Diary,

After the soccer game, Rodney joined Bunk Elvis for lunch. While we ate vegetable lasagna, garlic rolls, and salad, Lark and her dad compared their favorite soccer stars.

"Joe Stanford bends it better than Mick Linfield," Rodney argued.

"Dad, get real!" Lark said. "Nobody is better than Mick. He rules!"

"Lasagna, Rodney?" Ivy asked, holding out the tray.

Rodney rubbed his hands. "Pass it over here, love!" he said. "Lasagna is my favorite!"

"Really?" I asked across the table. "I thought your favorite dish was macaroni and cheese."

Rodney stuck his finger in his mouth and pretended to gag. "I wouldn't touch macaroni and cheese with a ten-foot cricket bat!" he said. "Who told you it was my favorite?"

"Your book did," I said. "It also said you love hiking. And boating. And—"

"Hate it!" Rodney interrupted. "The woods creep me out. And nothing makes me want to heave more than a rocky boat."

"But you used to row with your dad," Janelle said.

"Dad brought me along to keep the rowboat from tipping," Rodney said. "So he could stand up and fish."

"But," I started to say. "Your book says—"

"Total rubbish!" Rodney said. "It wasn't written by me. The bloke who wrote it made up most of it."

No wonder the book said nothing about soccer, I thought. *The guy who wrote it didn't have a clue!*

"How did you learn how to play soccer so well, Rodney?" Ashley asked.

"At the Sneddington School for Boys," Rodney said. "Only in England, we call it football. By the time I was thirteen, I was the school champ. Our team won a cabinet full of trophies."

"My team has won trophies, too, Dad," Lark said.

"I'll have to watch you play," Rodney said.

"When you have a concert in Santa Fe?" Lark asked.

"Forget the concert," Rodney declared. "Just tell me when you're playing, and I'm there."

"Really?" Lark asked. "Suuuuper!"

Janelle leaned over to me. "Mission accomplished," she whispered.

I'm sure there's a lot more that Lark and her dad will learn about each other, Diary. But they won't need my help!

Dear Diary,

I know I already wrote you today, Diary. But guess what? Electric Pink went to Stella with the tape. She listened to it, then sent a counselor to bring Venus to her office.

Diary, you should have seen those Venus girls. They looked totally shocked when Stella played them the tape.

"That's not really us!" Skye said. She pointed to Phoebe, Erin, and me. "They disguised their voices!"

"Nice try, Skye," Stella said. "But as I said before, Camp Rock 'n' Roll doesn't stand for pranks. Not only are they immature, they can be dangerous."

"Does that mean we're disqualified, too?" Skye asked.

"No," Stella said.

"What?" I heard myself gasp. How could *we* be disqualified and not Venus?

80

Twist and Shout

"I want *both* of your bands to compete in the Battle of the Bands," Stella said.

"You do?" Phoebe asked.

"Why?" Erin asked.

"All of the work here leads up to the Battle of the Bands," Stella said. "You should experience it, too. *But* you'll all have to help the roadies clear the stage and pack up. That means missing the end-of-summer party."

We all thanked Stella. Then we filed out of her office into the hall.

"We're still going to win, you know," Abigail said to us.

"We'll find out tomorrow," I said.

Venus turned and stalked away.

"Tomorrow!" Phoebe gasped.

"Omigosh!" Erin said. "We have to practice!"

And that's why I'd better stop writing, Diary. Wish me luck!

Chapter 12

Monday

Dear Diary,

Lark is still over the moon about her dad. But I'm kind of worried.

Today is the final round of the Battle of the Bands. What if Lark chokes in front of her dad again? It could spoil everything!

I tried not to think about it as we filed into the theater. This time, the place was decorated to the max. Balloons and banners were hanging everywhere. Rock music blasted from speakers as we took our seats.

A bunch of guys in the back of the theater were setting up huge lights and cameras. They were wearing RODNEY BEECHAM CONCERT TOUR jackets.

That's probably for Rodney's TV special, I thought. The special was going to be filmed tomorrow.

I looked around at the other bands. Everyone was totally stylin' and so were we. Janelle, Lark, and I were dressed in camouflage cargo pants, halter tops, and short combat boots. Lark and I wore camouflage bandannas on our heads. Janelle tied hers around her neck. She wanted to show off the green and pink streaks in her hair.

Ashley sat in the second row. She, Phoebe, and

Erin were dressed totally sixties, in plastic minidresses, white go-go boots, and big chunky jewelry shaped like daisies, hearts, even giant dice. Erin wore rose-colored shades with matching lipstick.

Ashley turned and gave me a thumbs-up sign. I gave her one, too. We were good to go!

"This is the moment we've all been waiting for!" Stella shouted onstage. "The Battle of the Bands!"

Everyone clapped, cheered, and stomped their feet.

"Today our judges have been joined by our favorite rocker," Stella announced. "Rodney Beecham!"

Rodney stood up from the judges' table and took a bow.

"As you all know, the focus of this last round is songwriting," Stella said. "And we'll begin with Crush!"

Omigosh! I thought. *We're first.*

I didn't realize how nervous I was until I got onstage. Everything was a big blur until I sat down behind my cans, buckets, and pails. I raised my drumsticks in the air and waited for Janelle to strum her guitar and shout, "One, two, three!"

Gripping my sticks, I exploded with my left arm and matched it with my right.

"'Just like you! Just like you!'" Janelle and I sang.

Lark shook her tambourine with one hand and gripped the mike with the other. As Lark sang, I listened for her voice to shake. It didn't. In fact, she sounded better than she ever had before!

"'It's just like you to make me smile! It's just like you to drive me wild!'" Lark sang.

I glanced at Rodney. He wasn't watching *me* this time. He was watching Lark—with a proud smile on his face!

Janelle played an awesome guitar solo at the end of the song. Then we lined up and took our bows.

"I was feeling the words, Crush," Clarence said. "Rock on with your funky selves!"

"I'm with Clarence," Sophie said. "Your lyrics were fun and fresh. Good job!"

So far, so good! I thought. *But there's still Terrence.*

"Your lyrics were quite good," he said. "I also see that Lark finally chilled out. Well done, Crush."

Stella announced our score. It was an *eight*!

"Do you believe it?" I shrieked backstage.

"That's the highest score we ever got," Lark said.

Janelle gave her guitar a twang. "How cool is that?" she said.

"Way cool!" I declared.

You know what's even cooler, Diary? We might even have a chance of winning!

Twist and Shout

Dear Diary,

Is it possible to have goose bumps on your teeth? Or between your toes? I was never so nervous.

My knees knocked together as I sat in the theater watching the other bands. The Corral Chicks performed a great country-rock song they wrote together. Stringz didn't sing but they composed a beautiful instrumental.

"I wish we'd go on already," Phoebe whispered. "This waiting is torture!"

The Corral Chicks got a score of seven. Stringz got a six. Terrence said one of the violins sounded like a cat with hair balls. Ouch!

"All-riiiight!" Stella announced. "I think we've been on this planet long enough. How about a trip to Venus?"

Skye, Tori, and Abigail bounced up. They were wearing their silver jumpsuits and matching space boots. Even their faces were painted silver this time.

Skye, Tori, and Abigail sang a song called "Out of This World." The words were really cute. And their bubble machine was back to normal again.

Everyone in the room seemed to like their song. Especially the judges. They gave Venus the highest score yet: a *ten*!

"Ten?" Phoebe squeaked.

"Now we have to get a ten, too," I whispered. "If we want to win."

"But that's a perfect score," Erin whispered.

"We can do it," I whispered back.

Then it was Electric Pink a Go-Go's turn.

I tried not to think about Venus as we climbed up on the stage. Erin sat down behind her keyboard. Phoebe and I stood side by side with our guitars.

"Remember," I murmured. "We can do it."

Erin began the opening melody. As we sang "Great to Know You," I saw mod daisies and hearts flashing on the stage wall. But when Jennifer projected pictures of friends at camp, the audience went wild.

"'Great to know you! Who would have guessed?'" we sang. "'My friendship with you would be the best!'"

Phoebe and I strummed the last few chords of the song. Then it was over. The audience cheered loudly as we bowed.

Sophie thought our song was "heartwarming." Clarence said we had a "foot-tapping beat." Even Terrence liked our lyrics. He called them "catchy."

We did it, I thought, squeezing Phoebe's and Erin's hands. *With those responses, we had to get—*

"Nine!" Stella announced. "Electric Pink a Go-Go gets a nine score."

Twist and Shout

My stomach dropped. I tried not to look, but I saw three faces smirking at us from the audience.

Three *silver* faces!

"Will our counselors tally up the scores of all four rounds?" Stella asked. "Then we can declare a winner."

Phoebe, Erin, and I picked up our instruments and trudged back to our seats.

"It's bad enough losing," Erin muttered. "But did we have to lose to Venus?"

"And now," Stella declared onstage, "the winner of the Battle of the Bands is—"

"We did our best," I said. "What more could we—"

"Electric Pink a Go-Go!" Stella announced.

What?

"Phoebe? Erin?" I asked. "Did she just say—"

"Electric Pink?" Erin squeaked.

"I . . . think . . . so," Phoebe said.

Everyone clapped and cheered. Jennifer ran over and hugged each of us. "You did it," she said. "You won!"

"But . . . how?" I asked.

"Venus had the highest score today," Jennifer said. "But your band had the highest total score."

Phoebe, Erin and I ran onstage. Stella and the judges were waiting for us with three trophies. They were shaped like electric guitars and had inscriptions that read: BEST BAND OF CAMP ROCK 'N' ROLL!

"Go Electric Pink!" I heard Mary-Kate shout.

I smiled as we waved our trophies in the air. Who would have thought things would turn out so awesome? Now we're best band *and* best friends. And that, Diary, is a winning combination!

Chapter 13

Tuesday

Dear Diary,

We won the Battle of the Bands, but we still had to clean up the theater.

But so did Venus.

"What could be worse than having to clean?" Erin grumbled as she swept the stage.

"Being disqualified?" I said.

"Oh, right!" Erin giggled.

We helped the roadies sweep, move amps, pack equipment, and turn all the seats up. When the work was done, we raced to the rec hall. Luckily, everyone was still partying!

There was a table full of hero sandwiches, salads, chips, and pitchers of lemonade to drink. Stella had even invited a DJ to spin discs. But the best part wasn't the DJ or the food. It was when Rodney and Lark sang a duet!

"Isn't it awesome?" Mary-Kate asked me. "Rodney is finally paying attention to Lark."

"It *is* awesome," I agreed. "But I think a dad should pay attention to his daughter even if she *doesn't* sing or play soccer."

Mary-Kate shrugged. "True. But it's a great start."

By the time we got back to Bunk Elvis we were all happy, tired, and little sad, too.

"I'm going to miss Camp Rock 'n' Roll," I said. "I can't believe we're going home on Friday."

"Camp isn't over yet," Ivy said. "We still have three more days of jam sessions."

"*And* we'll get to watch Rodney Beecham tape his new TV special," Janelle said. "Featuring Mary-Kate!"

That all happened last night, Diary. And today I'm so beat, I can hardly hold my pen. Which is okay, because I have to stop writing, anyway. Stella just brought Rodney Beecham into our bunk. Maybe he's here to talk to Lark—or to Mary-Kate—about the TV special.

Whatever it is, Diary, we'll find out!

Dear Diary,

As soon as Rodney, Doris, and Stella walked into Bunk Elvis I searched for my drumsticks.

"Is it time to shoot the TV special?" I asked.

Rodney whipped off his shades. "There's been a change of plans, love," he said.

"Rodney wants *Lark* to sing with him in the TV special," Doris said. "Her singing really wowed him yesterday."

Stella smiled at Lark. "You seemed a lot more comfortable onstage," she said. "We all think you're ready."

Lark's mouth dropped open. She stared at her father. "Are you *sure*, Dad?" she asked.

"Sure, I'm sure!" Rodney said. "You've got your dad's voice. And your mom's good looks!"

Lark smiled, and her eyes lit up. I was happy for her. But worried too.

Does this mean I won't be in the TV special?

It was as if Lark read my mind. "What about Mary-Kate, Dad?" she asked. "You asked her to be in the TV special, too."

"Mary-Kate will still be in the special!" Rodney said. "She'll play her buckets and cans exactly as planned."

Total relief!

"And you," Rodney said, pointing to Janelle. "Your guitar riffs completely brought down the house. How would you like to be in my TV special, too?"

Without a word Janelle fell to her knees and played air guitar.

"I guess that means yes!" Rodney chuckled. "Oh—don't bother learning the words to 'Lively Girl.' I picked a new song that's much better."

"What is it?" I asked.

"It's called," Rodney said, turning to Phoebe, "'Great to Know You!'"

"'Great to Know You?'" Phoebe gasped. "That's *my* song!"

"I really dug it!" Rodney said. "So much that I'd like to sing it, if you don't mind."

"I don't mind!" Phoebe said, her eyes sparkling.

"Just make sure you tell her if you change the lyrics," Erin teased.

Ashley and Erin hugged Phoebe. Rodney pointed to them, too.

"And you girls!" he said. "I could really use some groovy go-go dancers in the TV special. It goes with the theme of my special, 'Getting Mod with Rod!'"

The look on Ashley's face was pure shock. All she could say was, "Omigosh!"

"Our producer has picked a location down by the lake," Doris said. "We'll work on the song all day today, rehearse the TV special tomorrow, and shoot it on Thursday."

"Rock on, girls," Rodney said. Then he, Doris, and Stella walked out of the bunk.

We all stared at one another for what seemed like forever. Then we let out the biggest earsplitting shriek!

"Ivy's in the counselor's lounge," Erin said, after

we stopped jumping up and down and hugging one another. "Let's tell her the great news!"

We charged out of the bunk. But as the others ran ahead, Ashley and I fell behind.

"You know what, Mary-Kate?" Ashley asked. "I'm glad I let you talk me into Camp Rock 'n' Roll."

"Talk you into it?" I laughed. "Excuse me, but you were packing the minute I showed you the camp brochure!"

We hooked arms and made our way across the campgrounds.

This has been one amazing time, Diary. And it isn't over yet. Not only am I going to play drums for a major rock star on TV, all of my friends are going to be there with me. What could be better than that?

Camp Rock 'n' Roll doesn't only rock—it totally rules!

And so do we!

Dear Diary,

Okay, okay. I know what you're going to say, Diary (that is, if you could talk). Fortune-telling is not for real. It's all just a trick.

Even so, I just couldn't stop thinking about Bethany. Could she really predict the future?

Well, there was only one way I was going to find out.

I hurried over to her trailer at the carnival and went in to talk to her.

"Mary-Kate!" Bethany, the fortune teller, greeted me with a huge smile. "I'm so glad you came back! Sit down."

Bethany took out her Tarot cards and placed five of them down on the table.

"Hmm. This is interesting," Bethany said, pointing to

a card. "Somebody is going to give you a present. And it looks like something you really want."

"What is it?" I asked.

"I don't know," she said. "But the cards say you're going to be receiving a present from someone very soon."

I shook my head. "It's not my birthday. And Christmas is two months away. Who would give me a present?" I asked.

Bethany didn't know—that was all she saw.

After I left her, I went back to my dorm. When I arrived, Phoebe and Ginger were hanging out with my roommate, Campbell.

As I flopped down on my bed, Campbell handed me an envelope. "This is for you, Mary-Kate," she said. "It showed up an hour ago. Somebody stuck it under the door."

I took the envelope and opened it. Inside were two tickets to the New Hampshire College women's basketball finals, featuring my favorite team—the Hampshire Hoops!

The game was totally sold out. The tickets were impossible to get. And suddenly I had two of them! "Incredible!" Campbell exclaimed. "Who sent them?"

I peered in the envelope for a note, but there was nothing else in it except the tickets. I looked at the outside of the envelope. My name was printed on it in block letters. But there was no return address.

That's when I remembered Bethany.

"I can't believe it," I said. "She predicted this would happen!"

"Who?" Phoebe wanted to know.

"Bethany," I told her. "I went back to the carnival today. She read my fortune again and said I'd be getting a gift. And here it is."

"But how could she have known?" Ginger asked.

I stared at the tickets. "I have no idea."

Diary, I never thought I believed in any of this supernatural stuff. But now I'm not so sure . . .

Dear Diary,

My friend, Jill, looked a little worried today, when I finally dragged her to the afternoon performance of the circus. I knew our article about the circus for the school newspaper would be great. I just wished that Jill would relax, so she could take some good pictures.

The clowns were a total hoot. The funniest of them all were a man and a woman who played a married couple. I've never laughed so hard in my life. When their act was over, I clapped until my hands hurt.

"I can't wait to interview them!" I whispered to Jill, after they left the arena.

"Interview them?" Jill said, biting her lower lip. "Oh, I don't know. I mean, do you really want to interview some clowns?"

"Why not?" I asked, getting up to leave. "They were the best part of the show!"

"Yeah," Jill said. "But all the magic disappears when they take off their makeup, you know? It's all about make-believe. It would ruin things to see them without their noses and stuff."

"Then we can talk to them before they take off their makeup," I told her. "Come on. The dressing rooms are right over there!"

That's when Jill grabbed my arm. "Ashley!" she cried. "No way!" And she actually dragged me out of the tent!

Once again, Jill was acting totally strange.

Then, I finally figured it out. Jill must be scared of clowns!

"Look, Jill," I told her. "If you're . . . well . . . nervous around the clowns, I understand. My cousin Jeremy has been scared of clowns ever since he was little. Lots of people are. It's nothing to be ashamed of . . ."

Jill gasped. "Scared of them?"

"Maybe I can help," I offered.

"Believe me, Ashley, you don't understand," she said seriously. "There's absolutely nothing you can do to help."

Diary, what is it with Jill? One minute, she's nice and perfectly okay. Then as soon as we get to the circus, she totally freaks out and seems to have a big secret.

I'm going to find out what she's hiding!

WIN A SUPER COOL ELECTRIC GUITAR!

One Grand Prize Winner will receive a

FENDER Electric Guitar

Mail to: **TWO OF A KIND**
ELECTRIC GUITAR SWEEPSTAKES
c/o HarperEntertainment
Attention: Children's Marketing Department
10 East 53rd Street, New York, NY 10022

No purchase necessary.

Name: _____

Address: _____

City: _____ State: _____ Zip: _____

Phone: _____ Age: _____

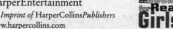

HarperEntertainment
An Imprint of HarperCollins*Publishers*
www.harpercollins.com

Two Of A Kind
Electric Guitar Sweepstakes

OFFICIAL RULES:

1. No purchase or payment necessary to enter or win.

2. How to Enter. To enter, complete the official entry form or hand print your name, address, age, and phone number along with the words *"Two Of A Kind* Electric Guitar Sweepstakes" on a 3" x 5" card and mail to: *Two Of A Kind* Electric Guitar Sweepstakes, c/o HarperEntertainment, Attn: Children's Marketing Department, 10 East 53rd Street, New York, NY 10022. Entries must be received no later than October 30, 2004. Enter as often as you wish, but each entry must be mailed separately. One entry per envelope. Partially completed, illegible, or mechanically reproduced entries will not be accepted. Sponsor is not responsible for lost, late, mutilated, illegible, stolen, postage due, incomplete, or misdirected entries. All entries become the property of Dualstar Entertainment Group, LLC, and will not be returned.

3. Eligibility. Sweepstakes open to all legal residents of the United States (excluding Colorado and Rhode Island), who are between the ages of five and fifteen on October 30, 2004 excluding employees and immediate family members of HarperCollins Publishers, Inc., ("HarperCollins"), Warner Bros.Pictures Inc. ("Warner"), Parachute Properties and Parachute Press, Inc., and their respective subsidiaries and affiliates, officers, directors, shareholders, employees, agents, attorneys, and other representatives and their immediate families (individually and collectively, 'Parachute'), Dualstar Entertainment Group, LLC, and its subsidiaries and affiliates, officers, directors, shareholders, employees, agents, attorneys, and other representatives and their immediate families (individually and collectively, "Dualstar"), and their respective parent companies, affiliates, subsidiaries, advertising, promotion and fulfillment agencies, and the persons with whom each of the above are domiciled. All applicable federal, state and local laws and regulations apply. Offer void where prohibited or restricted by law.

4. Odds of Winning. Odds of winning depend on the total number of entries received. Approximately 300,000 sweepstakes announcements published. All prizes will be awarded. Winners will be randomly drawn on or about November 15, 2004, by HarperCollins, whose decision is final. Potential winners will be notified by mail and will be required to sign and return an affidavit of eligibility and release of liability within 14 days of notification. Prizes won by minors will be awarded to parent or legal guardian who must sign and return all required legal documents. By acceptance of their prize, winner consents to the use of their name, photograph, likeness, and biographical information by HarperCollins, Parachute, Dualstar, and for publicity purposes without further compensation except where prohibited.

5. Grand Prize. One Grand Prize Winner will win a Fender electric guitar. Approximate retail value of prize totals $300.00.

6. Prize Limitations. All prizes will be awarded. Only one prize will be awarded per individual, family, or household. Prizes are non-transferable and cannot be sold or redeemed for cash. No cash substitute is available. Any federal, state, or local taxes are the responsibility of the winner. Sponsor may substitute prize of equal or greater value, if necessary, due to availability.

7. Additional terms: By participating, entrants agree a) to the official rules and decisions of the judges, which will be final in all respects; and to waive any claim to ambiguity of the official rules and b) to release, discharge, and hold harmless HarperCollins, Warner, Parachute, Dualstar, and their respective parent companies, affiliates, subsidiaries, employees and representatives and advertising, promotion and fulfillment agencies from and against any and all liability or damages associated with acceptance, use, or misuse of any prize received or participation in any sweepstakes-related activity or participation in this Sweepstakes.

8. Dispute Resolution. Any dispute arising from this Sweepstakes will be determined according to the laws of the State of New York, without reference to its conflict of law principles, and the entrants consent to the personal jurisdiction of the State and Federal courts located in New York County and agree that such courts have exclusive jurisdiction over all such disputes.

9. Winner Information. To obtain the name of the winner, please send your request and a self-addressed stamped envelope (residents of Vermont may omit return postage) to *Two Of A Kind* Electric Guitar Winner, c/o HarperEntertainment, 10 East 53rd Street, New York, NY 10022 by December 15, 2005.

10. Sweepstakes Sponsor: HarperCollins Publishers, Inc. Fender© Musical Instruments Corporation is not affiliated, connected or associated with this Sweepstakes in any manner and bears no responsibility for the administration of this Sweepstakes.

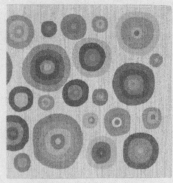